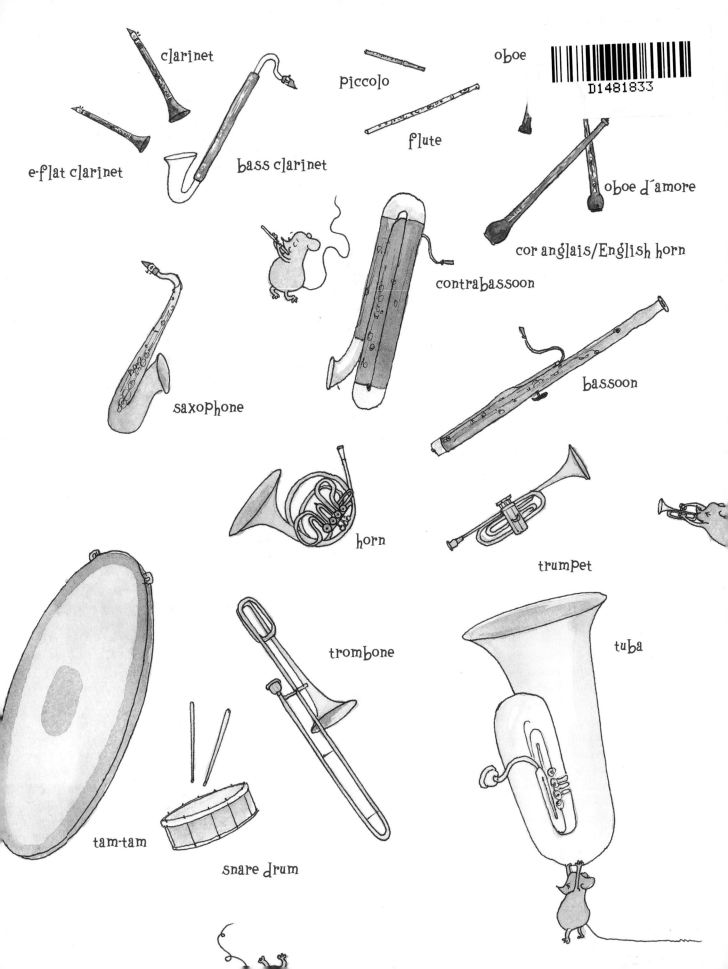

For children of all ages:

a first step to a lifelong enjoyment of music.

Vladimir Ashkenazy,

Conductor Laureate

of the Iceland Symphony Orchestra is

Patron of the Maximus Musicus project.

Maximus Musicus

visits
the orchestra

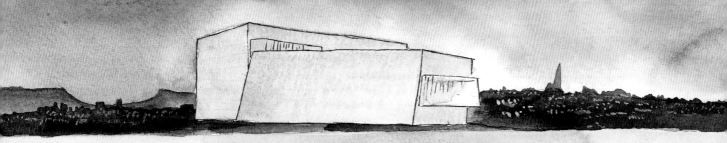

Hallfríður Ólafsdóttir
Þórarinn Már Baldursson

Translated by Daði Kolbeinsson

animusia

Maximus Musics visits the orchestra

Text © 2008 Hallfríður Ólafsdóttir

Illustrations © 2008 Þórarinn Már Baldursson

Design: Margrét E. Laxness

Soundtrack design: Hallfríður Ólafsdóttir and Georg Magnússon

Color: Pixel prentþjónusta

Printed in China by Pettit Network Inc.

First published as

Maxímús Músíkús heimsækir hljómsveitina

🎼 Forlagið hf., Reykjavík 2008

This worldwide English edition copyright © 2012 Music Word Media Group.
Music Word Media® is a Registered Service Mark of
Music Word Media Group, Ltd. in the United States of America.

animusia

An Animusia book

www.animusia.com

Music audio:

Producer sound engineer: Georg Magnússon

Tonmeister: Bjarni Rúnar Bjarnason, Bernd Obermayr

Sound engineers for Maxi's Song: Magnús Árni Öder Kristjánsson and Jósef Smith

Recording venues: Háskólabíó and FIH Studios, Reykjavík 2007

ISBN 9781937330170

DOI 10.5726/ 9781937330040

Library of Congress Control Number: 2011940097

An iPad edition of this book is available at www.musicwordmedia.net.

Follow Maxi's exploits at http://www.maximusmusicus.com
and on Facebook at Maximus Musicus

One winter's night, a mouse scurried through the snow.
His name was Maximus Musicus.

All day he had enjoyed himself, exploring the busy town streets,
but now he was positively chilly. "Ooh, this wind is almost
freezing my tail off," said Maximus, curling
his long tail close to his body with
a shiver. He ran into the shelter
of a sky-high building just
as a door opened. The
mouse shot through
the gap before
it slammed
shut again.

It was dark inside, but Maximus Musicus didn't mind at all, and he soon found a little hole to rest in. "Well, Maxi," he said to himself, stroking his whiskers, "this seems a good place to rest till morning. Good night."

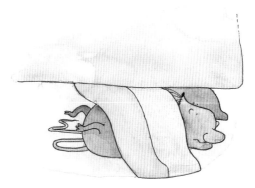

Early next day, Maximus was woken by a strange noise.

Plink!

Maxi sat up. He peeped out of his hole, and towering way above him he saw ...

**Plink, Plinnk, Plinnnk.
Pllieeiiinnnk!**

... a large golden harp with an enormous number of strings – far too many to count.

Maximus Musicus stared at the harp and thought, "What luck! That's a musical instrument that people play, just like in the stories old Great-Grandpa Musicus used to tell us. I must find somewhere to hide so I can listen."

The lady with the harp was very busy tuning her instrument and didn't notice Maxi. It was taking her rather a long time because each string had its own special note, and she had to tighten or loosen them, one at a time, until they sounded just right.

All of a sudden, a loud squeak made Maxi jump. He almost fell into a box that lay on the floor. "Well now, what can this be?" he thought as he peered into the case. Three shiny tubes lay there.

"Interesting!" said the mouse, but he had to jump quickly out of the way when a neat hand reached down, carefully took the tubes out of the case, and joined them together to make one long pipe. It was a silver flute. The flautist lifted the instrument to her lips and blew softly into it.

Maximus was entranced by the soothing sound of the flute ...

... until he heard a disturbing new sound.

Purrrr, purrrrurrr!

Oh no! A cat!

Maximus Musicus felt a sinking feeling in his stomach.

Purrrrpurrrrpurrrrr...

Now Maxi realised that it couldn't be a cat. A tall man stood nearby, making the strange sound with something he pressed to his mouth. "What on earth is he doing?" thought the mouse. "Surely only serious instruments are allowed here." Then the tall man lifted up a gleaming trumpet. He had just been loosening up his lips by blowing into the mouthpiece.

More musicians arrived, carrying shiny brass instruments. Maximus stared at them all in wonder, but he was even more surprised when several large drops of water fell on him.

Gracious! Is it raining indoors?

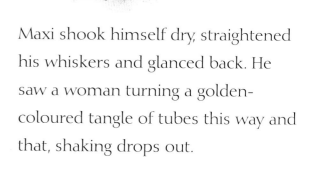

Maxi shook himself dry, straightened his whiskers and glanced back. He saw a woman turning a golden-coloured tangle of tubes this way and that, shaking drops out.

Maxi leapt out of the puddle, then heard a strange rumbling noise.

The ground shook. Maximus trembled from head to toe.

"Oh, there's much too much going on here. It's an earthquake!" he thought to himself. He looked up terrified, and saw what he thought was a grizzly bear standing over him roaring.

Grurrr, grurrr, grurrr

But the din suddenly stopped. There was no bear, just a bearded man leaning over a gigantic curvy brown box. Maxi quickly slipped aside as the double-bass player continued scrubbing the thick strings with his bow.

More and more musicians arrived, but when they started to play the air was filled with a deafening jumble of sounds. "What a cacophony," said Maxi to himself. "Don't these people know how to play real music?"

He watched a violin player grip the end of her violin and twist a peg while she ran her bow across a string so the sound wandered up and down.

Maximus Musicus stroked his whiskers and wondered. This was something he definitely wanted to try for himself. He picked out his longest, finest whisker. "This should sound great," he thought, "but what can I use as a stick?" He grabbed his long, sleek tail and tried stroking his whisker, but he couldn't make any sound at all.

Maxi was most disappointed. Then he overheard two violinists talking together.

The violinist took the block of rosin and rubbed his bow on it. Then he carried on playing.

"That's very interesting," thought the mouse, and scuttled across to the rosin. It was a strange and sticky brown block, but Maxi ran his tail over it all the same. He tried stroking his whisker again ...

... and now it began to vibrate and sing.

"Brilliant!" thought Maxi and played and played. The notes went up as he stretched his whisker and down when he let it go slack.

Like most mice, Maximus Musicus preferred the high notes. He tugged harder and harder, and the notes became higher and higher and sounded even sweeter to his ear. Maxi was spellbound by the wonderful sounds.

But then ...

Ouch!

... his whisker snapped!

Tears welled up in his eyes. "That hurt", sniffed Maxi. "Becoming
a musician is no walk in the park!"

But wait – what was that? He forgot the pain when he heard a
clatter behind the violinist.

Maxi turned round and saw a slice of wood fall onto the floor. Several others lay nearby. They were mouse-sized planks, but all very thin at one end.

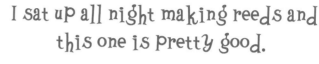

Oh dear, this reed is useless too.

I sat up all night making reeds and this one is pretty good.

The bassoon player put the double reed between his lips and blew. A strange croak came from his mouth, but then he pushed the reed onto a narrow, hook-shaped pipe attached to his instrument, and the dignified tone of the bassoon emerged when he blew.

The clarinet player licked yet another piece of wood as if it were a lollipop and held it to the top end of her instrument. She put a metal clip over it and screwed it tight. Then she blew into her instrument and said, "Yes, that's much better."

Yet another peculiar noise could be heard, but it wasn't a musical instrument this time.

It was Maxi's empty tummy rumbling. He looked around and was pleased to see a piece of cheese on a little shelf. Maxi made straight for it.

No-one noticed Maxi as he climbed up onto the shelf. It was full of odd things – gadgets, tools and – cheese! Maximus Musicus licked his lips and took a good bite.

Yuck!

What a disappointment. It wasn't cheese at all. It was a spongy soft, yellow and salty foam rubber, and not at all good to eat. Some thin slivers of cane lay on it like a row of little princesses on a soft cushion.

   The oboe player turned round and took one of the reeds. He sucked it, blew through it and made it crow like the bassoon player had done earlier. Then he pushed it a little way into a tiny hole in the end of his instrument and blew into it. His fingers moved very quickly, producing cascades of notes running up and down. Maxi listened in amazement to all the different sounds the instruments made.

Suddenly, everything went quiet. The violin player at the very front of
the orchestra stood up and pointed his bow straight at Maxi.
"Oh no, what next?" Maxi wondered horrified.

Wind and brass, tune up please.

M. RAVEL
BOLERO

The oboe player poked a button on the gadget that Maxi was hiding
behind, took a deep breath and blew a very, very, very long note.
All the wind and brass players blew into their instruments
and imitated the oboe's note. Then the string players
tuned all their strings.
Just then another person, without an instrument,
joined the group. He had nothing but a short, sharp
stick. He shook hands with the leader of the
orchestra, then said to all, "Good morning,
we'll begin with the Bolero." He lifted his
hands and there was total silence. All
the musicians were watching the conductor, so
Maximus Musicus jumped quietly
down to the floor.

The conductor lifted his hands very slightly further and then let them gently fall and gracefully bounce up again. A drummer began beating his drum very quietly, tapping in time to the conductor's movements.

Rumm patetee rumm patetee rumm pumm pumm patetee rumm patetee patetee patetee

String players plucked their strings — and then the sound of the flute came drifting over the drumbeats. Maximus held his breath. The music was so quiet, yet expressive, that he had to listen intently, as if someone was whispering a secret in his ear. Maxi felt as though he was floating on gently swaying clouds.

When the flute had ended, the clarinet played the same tune again. Maxi was delighted. He wanted to hear that tune again and again.

Then it was the bassoon's turn, but the music became a little sadder, almost as if the bassoon was crying.

The drummer kept up his beat, and the sad tune passed to a much smaller clarinet. Maximus Musicus listened to the heartbreaking melody. He thought of Great-Grandpa Musicus, who had told him about people and their wonderful music. The old mouse used to tell great stories from the days when he was a house-mouse in the home of the city's most famous composer. The rooms had been filled with music day and night. Maxi really missed his Great-Grandpa.

But something in the harmony promised happier times. Maxi didn't realise immediately where the new sound was coming from, because the violinists didn't lift up their instruments. Instead, they plucked them like guitars.

A strange oboe with a bulge on the end was playing in the middle of the orchestra and Maxi realised that everyone wanted to play the beautiful melody, sometimes a solitary soloist, sometimes in a group.

The trumpet played a duet with the flute ...

... but the big tenor saxophone and the small soprano saxophone each had a chance to play on their own.

And when the horn played, the celeste and two small piccolo flutes joined in. The sound was like nothing Maxi had heard before.

Then the oboes joined the clarinets ...

... the trombone played alone ...

... and all the woodwind played together.

At last, it was the violins' turn to play the tune. Now the players lifted their instruments to their shoulders and drew their bows over the strings in long, graceful strokes. Timeless notes entwined through the air like magic threads weaving an invisible web.

Oh Maximus Musicus, this is by far the most wonderful sound you have ever heard!

The whole orchestra now played together as one, and they seemed to be blowing, beating and bowing as vigorously as they could. Some of the wind players were even becoming rather red in the face.

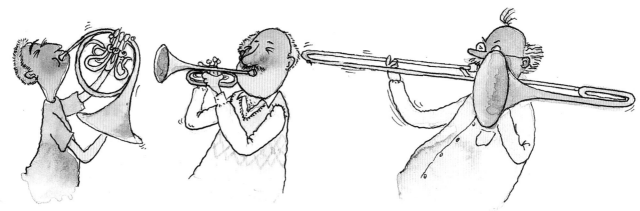

The noise was deafening. It was really too much for a little mouse. Maxi made a dash for the stage curtains, fastened his claws into the plush velvet and started to climb.

Up and up he went, higher and higher, until the volume was more bearable for little mouse ears. He looked down from his high perch over the heads of the musicians. There were almost a hundred of them, and some were rather bald!

The music grew even louder. Maxi felt faint. He lost his grip and fell, down, down, a long way down ...

Oh-oh! This doesn't look too good!

... but his fall was broken when he landed on a gigantic slide. He slithered to a halt and opened his eyes. He was inside a very large cavern of shiny metal. And there was absolutely no way he could climb back out.

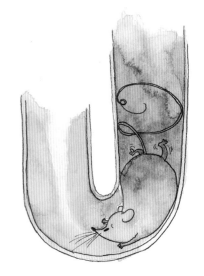

The orchestra stopped playing. The conductor tapped his stand with his stick. "Thorburn, what's the problem?" he asked.

I don't know, Maestro. I simply can't seem to get any sound out of my tuba.

The tuba player sighed, took a deep breath and blew hard into his instrument. Maxi felt a hot wind tickle his toes. He had indeed landed inside the tuba!

"Help, what do I do now?" thought the trembling little mouse. He didn't want to think about what might happen next.

The tuba player took another breath and blew powerfully once again, but little happened.

Then the tuba player filled his lungs with air and blew as hard as he possibly could.

Maxi felt an immense push and flew out of the tuba, soaring through the air accompanied by a deep bellow.

Maxi was heading for the trombones just as the orchestra began playing again ...

The trombone slides were flashing in and out and he managed to grab one. What fun!

But again the noise was too much for him and he let go ...

... flying onto and upsetting a whole row of percussion instruments ...

CrashBangBoomCrashBong!
Clang! Tickticktick,
Zingzingzingzingzzzinnngg...

... just as the conductor cut off the orchestra's final chord. The surprised musicians turned round to see what on earth was going on behind them. Then they all started to laugh. What a joke!

"Break!" announced the conductor.

Everybody stood up, stretched, and left the stage.

Oh, I could do with a nice cup of tea!

Maximus heaved a sigh of relief and straightened his whiskers. He decided to follow the people and see if he could find something to eat.

After their break, the musicians started playing again, but Maxi stayed backstage nibbling on some crumbs he had found.

Some time later the rehearsal finished and the musicians packed up their instruments and went home.

Maximus was exhausted. He spotted a soft carpet under a big drum, and decided it would be a good place to curl up and have a nap. He cleaned his whiskers, lay down and soon he was snoring.

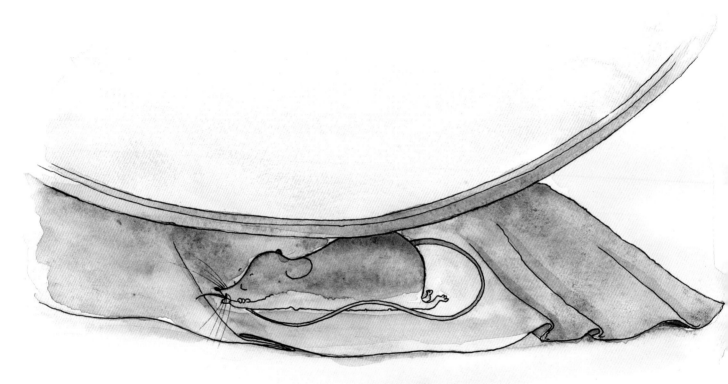

Maxi slept and slept.

He didn't wake up when the musicians came back.

He didn't wake up when the audience came into the concert hall.

He didn't even wake up when the audience started clapping as the musicians walked on stage.

No, Maximus Musicus was fast asleep.

Booumm!!!

Maxi nearly jumped out of his skin as the concert began with
a thunderous bang on the big bass drum. It was like the end
of the world!

Maxi leapt to his feet as the air filled with the sound of
blaring trumpets. Brass players and percussionists stood on
the stage playing majestic music. The concert hall was full of
people, and spotlights lit the smartly-dressed musicians.
Maximus Musicus was awestruck by the magnificent music,
and his heart beat faster with the heroic tones.

The fanfare ended and
Maxi clapped till his paws
were sore.
When the rest of the
orchestra came back on
stage, Maxi took the
opportunity to creep out into
the audience. Sitting right in
the middle of all that racket
was no place for a mouse,
that's for sure!
The hall fell silent as
the orchestra
prepared for the
next piece.

And then the whole symphony orchestra played together.

Maximus Musicus swayed back and forth with the music. In his mind he travelled over oceans and crossed continents to visit exotic lands until his head was swimming.

There was a moment's silence after the last note. The children who sat closest to Maxi looked at each other and smiled happily, then started clapping, along with everyone else in the audience.

The conductor waved for the orchestra to stand up – first the soloists, one at a time, and then the rest of the group. He then gracefully accepted a bouquet and left the stage.

But the audience kept on clapping!

Finally, they got their way. The conductor came back on stage with a spring in his step and waved his hands. The musicians lifted their instruments and launched into their encore – everyone's favourite – *On Sprengisandur.*

And what a gallop! Maximus heard beating hooves and neighing trumpets, while regal horns reminded him of the wind blowing over the highlands. It was a song about a rider and horse on a thrilling dash across wild countryside.

There was absolute pandemonium when the orchestra finished playing. The audience stood up, clapped, whistled and stamped. The musicians rose to their feet and the conductor bowed again and again.

Then it was all over.

Maxi was so full of joy he could hardly move. He watched the musicians shaking hands as they left the stage, and the audience filing through the exit doors.

"What a great day," thought Maximus Musicus as he scampered backstage. "Now I have stories to match the tales of Great-Grandpa Musicus. I'm going to nestle down here in this double bass and wait and see what happens tomorrow."

The End

Did you know?

The harp has 46 strings. The shortest one is the length of a toothpick, the longest one the height of a man.

Water collects inside wind instruments when humidity in the players' breath condenses....

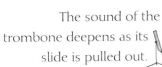

The bows of string instruments are strung with horsehair. Rosin is made from wood resin. It is rubbed on the bow hair to help it bite and produce sound.

The sound of oboes, bassoons and clarinets is made by thin slivers of vibrating cane. Clarinet reeds can be bought ready-made but most oboe and bassoon players make and scrape their own reeds.

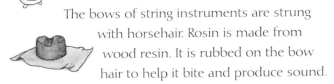

Flutes belong to the woodwind family. Originally they were wooden, but now are usually made of silver or other metals.

Timpani and drums are covered with animal skin or manmade membrane.

The sound of the trombone deepens as its slide is pulled out.

Horn players keep their right hand inside the bell of their instrument and can use it to adjust the tone and pitch of notes.

The violinist at the very front of the group is called the leader or concertmaster and is responsible for leading the orchestra and ensuring that it plays both in time and in tune.

The conductor's stick is called a baton.

Oboists tune the orchestra by playing the note A. They often use an electronic instrument to confirm the exact pitch of the note.

The celesta or celeste is a keyboard instrument with metal bars like a xylophone, struck by felt hammers. Its name is derived from its heavenly sound.

Violins, violas, cellos and basses have four strings, though basses can have five. Large instruments and long strings produce deep sounds, small instruments and short strings high-pitched tones.

Maxi's Song

Tune: Hallfríður Ólafsdóttir
Words: HÓ and PMB
Translation: Dadi Kolbeinsson

Allegro leggiero ♩. = 120

Max - i - mus Mu - si - cus, went in-side a ve-ry large house, in-to'a hole he quick-ly crept, cud-dled up and sound-ly slept. Max - i, Max - i, Max - i, Max - i mouse, hap - pi-ly ex - plor - ing the huge con-cert house. Max - i-mus Mu - si-cus, mu - sic mouse. *whistle*

meno mosso ♩ = 104

Sweet - ly sings the sym - pho - ny, heart - felt strings in har - mo - ny.

hum to the melody and imitate playing string instruments

Drum-sticks beat and bold-ly bu-gles call, bring-ing forth a sun-ny

smile on all. Max-i-mus Mu-si-cus, mu-sic mouse. *whistle*

Max-i-mus Mu-si-cus 'bout mu-sic is so cu-ri-ous.

con-cert o-ver, mu-si-cians stand, au-dience claps, bra-vo for the band! Max-i, Max-i,

Max-i, Max-i mouse, hap-pi-ly ex-plor-ing the huge con-cert house.

Max-i-mus Mu-si-cus, mu-sic mouse. *whistle*

©Hallfríður Ólafsdóttir, 2007

The Authors

Hallfríður Ólafsdóttir is the principal flautist of the Iceland Symphony Orchestra. Haffí has always been a bookworm. In her opinion symphonic music is the coolest thing on earth but she also has fun playing strange old flutes and whistles. The "ð" in Hallfríður's name is an Icelandic letter, pronounced like the voiced "th".

Þórarinn Már Baldursson is a violist in the Iceland Symphony Orchestra. Tóti has been drawing since he was a wee boy. He is also interested in traditional Icelandic culture, and is himself an accomplished bard. The "Þ" in Þórarinn's name is an Icelandic letter, pronounced like the unvoiced "th".

The Music:

Boléro by the French composer Maurice Ravel is based on a recurring theme set over a steady rhythm on the snaredrum, derived from the Spanish dance, bolero. Only a few instruments begin the piece, more are gradually added until at its conclusion, the whole orchestra is playing.

The beginning and the end of the first movement of Beethoven's Fifth Symphony is heard in the background as Maxi rests backstage. Probably the most famous theme of all time, the unyielding knock of Fate on the composer's door.

Fanfare for the Common Man, by the American composer, Aaron Copland is a fanfare in honor of ordinary people, as opposed to the many fanfares written for nobility and royalty in olden times.

On Sprengisandur (Á Sprengisandi) by the Icelandic songwriter Sigvaldi S. Kaldalóns is one of the country's most popular songs. Being ISO's favourite encore, it is frequently heard on the Iceland Symphony Orchestra's foreign tours, a galloping "tour de force" arranged colourfully by a former trumpeter and conductor of the orchestra, Páll Pampichler Pálsson.

The Performers

The Iceland Symphony Orchestra was established in 1950 and consists of around 90 players. The ISO performs mainly in Reykjavik but frequently tours abroad as well as within Iceland. Each year, the orchestra gives many school, infant school and family concerts.

To find out more about Maximus Musicus and the Iceland Symphony Orchestra go to www.sinfonia.is/Maxi or www.maximusmusicus.com.

Rumon Gamba was the principal conductor of the Iceland Symphony Orchestra when the music for this book was recorded. When a little boy in England, he used to wake up his Mum and Dad very early in the morning by practising his cello. Now he travels far and wide conducting symphony orchestras, while at home he is an enthusiastic cook much appreciated by his family.

Stella Arman narrates the story. Stella comes from a large family of musicians in England and has been a singer since childhood. She now performs in concert and in church, and trains singers and speakers in Austria and the UK.

Rannveig Káradóttir sings *Maxi's Song* with the Mouseband. Rannsl sings all kinds of music and as a young girl also played the flute. Now her favourite is the opera where she gets to wear colourful dresses.

The Mouseband consists of: Hallfríður Ólafsdóttir, flute, Ármann Helgason, clarinet, Ásgeir Steingrímsson, trumpet, Sigrún Eðvaldsdóttir, violin, Zbigniew Dubik, violin, Jónína Auður Hilmarsdóttir, viola, Bryndís Björgvinsdóttir, cello, Richard Korn, doublebass and Pétur Grétarsson, percussion.

Acknowledgements

Vladimir and Þórunn Ashkenazy, Ármann Helgason, Daði Kolbeinsson, Georg Magnússon, Guðrún Dalía Salómonsdóttir, Jane Smee, Magnea Árnadóttir, Malcolm Holloway, Rachel Wright, Rumon Gamba, Tómas Þorvaldsson.

Collaborators

Iceland Symphony Orchestra, State Fund for the Arts in Iceland, Icelandic Musician's Union, Icelandic Ministry of Education, Reykjavik City Arts Fund, Iceland State Radio, ISO Orchestra Members.

SINFÓNÍUHLJÓMSVEIT
ÍSLANDS

viola

violin

double bass

cello

harp

celesta
or celeste

bass drum

tympani

cymbals